PIRATE SCHOOL

Shiver Me, Shipwreck!

by Brian James
illustrated by Jennifer Zivoin

Grosset & Dunlap

For furry pirate pal Mitzie!—BJ

To my parents, for teaching me how
to avoid life's shipwrecks.— JZ

GROSSET & DUNLAP
Published by the Penguin Group
Penguin Group (USA) Inc., 375 Hudson Street, New York, New York 10014, USA
Penguin Group (Canada), 90 Eglinton Avenue East, Suite 700,
Toronto, Ontario M4P 2Y3, Canada
(a division of Pearson Penguin Canada Inc.)
Penguin Books Ltd., 80 Strand, London WC2R 0RL, England
Penguin Group Ireland, 25 St. Stephen's Green, Dublin 2, Ireland
(a division of Penguin Books Ltd.)
Penguin Group (Australia), 250 Camberwell Road, Camberwell, Victoria 3124, Australia
(a division of Pearson Australia Group Pty. Ltd.)
Penguin Books India Pvt. Ltd., 11 Community Centre,
Panchsheel Park, New Delhi—110 017, India
Penguin Group (NZ), 67 Apollo Drive, Rosedale, North Shore 0632, New Zealand
(a division of Pearson New Zealand Ltd.)
Penguin Books (South Africa) (Pty.) Ltd., 24 Sturdee Avenue,
Rosebank, Johannesburg 2196, South Africa

Penguin Books Ltd., Registered Offices:
80 Strand, London WC2R 0RL, England

Library of Congress Control Number: 2008020701

ISBN 978-0-448-44888-6   10 9 8 7 6 5 4 3 2 1

Chapter 1
Shipshape!

"Broken barnacles!" I hollered. "This is going to take forever."

There were loose boards sticking up all over the deck of the *Sea Rat*. We'd been ordered to fix them by our teacher, Rotten Tooth.

Rotten Tooth was always telling us that those chores he always ordered us to do were Pirate School lessons. Sometimes, I wasn't so sure. But Rotten Tooth wasn't only our teacher. He was also the first mate of the *Sea Rat*. Plus, he was the meanest pirate to ever sail the seas. That meant we had to listen to him or we'd be shark bait.

"I guess we better get started," I said. "Orders be orders."

"Arrr! I'd like to order Rotten Face to walk the plank!" Aaron grumbled.

"Arrr? That would only get us into trouble," Gary said. He was my best mate at Pirate School, and he didn't like getting into trouble.

"Aye, let's get to work," Vicky said with a groan. Then she picked up a hammer and started hammering.

Aaron covered his ears with both hands. "Arrr! Do you have to make such a racket?" he shouted. "You're going to wake every fish in the sea!"

Vicky stopped hammering and huffed.

She was Aaron's twin sister. They both had the same dark hair and dark eyes. Only, her eyes got darker and madder whenever Aaron complained.

"You heard Rotten Tooth," she said. "We have to make sure every nail on the whole entire deck is hammered in all the way."

"Aye, I heard him!" Aaron told her. "But he didn't say you had to be so loud about it!"

Vicky stomped her foot. Then she made a grumpy face. "Well, Captain Big Mouth, hammering is noisy business!" she told her brother.

"Aye," Inna said. "Plus, it's yucky business!"

Inna stood up and looked at her dress. It was all dirty where she had been kneeling on the grimy deck. That made her steaming mad! She was the only pirate kid in the world who hated getting dirty.

"Aye, and ouchy business, too!" Gary said after he hammered his thumb by mistake. I shook my head and tried not to giggle. Sometimes Gary could be one clumsy pirate!

"Arrr, it's not so bad," I said, trying to lift their sails. I didn't like

it when my mates moaned and groaned. "Besides," I said, "taking care of the ship is also very important business."

"Aye?" Vicky asked.

"Aye." I nodded. "It says so in the pirate code." I'd lived on a pirate ship all nine and three-quarters years of my life, so I knew all about the pirate code. "It says every pirate should take care of their ship just like they'd take care of a baby."

My mates made *oohs* and *aahs* and went back to work. I was hammering nails by the railing when I saw another ship sailing on the horizon.

"Great sails!" I said, and pointed at the ship.

My mates rushed over and took a peek. We didn't see many other ships on the open seas.

"Arrr! Do you think it's a pirate ship?" Inna asked.

"Arrr! Do you think it's a rival pirate ship?" Gary asked.

Inna GULPED!

She liked rival pirates even less than she liked getting dirty!

"Let's see," I said. I took my spyglass out of my coat pocket and spied on the other ship. "It's a pirate ship, all right," I said. I could tell by the flag.

"A good pirate ship or a bad pirate ship?" Inna asked.

I looked for a name on the side of the ship.

Then it was my turn to gulp! My timbers

started shaking and shivering when I read the name. "It's called the *Bone Rattler*," I said.

Inna and Gary DOUBLE GULPED because that was one scary name.

But Aaron and Vicky didn't gulp at all. In fact, they started jumping around and clapping!

"The *Bone Rattler* is the ship we were on before we came to Pirate School," Vicky explained.

"Blimey! That sure is a spooky name," Gary said.

"Aye! When I'm a pirate captain, there's no way I'll give my ship a spooky name," Inna said. "I'm going to call my ship the *Pretty Sea Princess*."

I rolled my eyes.

"Arrr! Let's go tell Captain Stinky Beard!" Vicky said. "Maybe we can change course to meet them."

"Aye," we all agreed. Then we raced off to find the cap'n and tell him the good news. It sure beat hammering all those nails!

Chapter 2
Ahoy at Sea!

"Ahoy, me lil' shipmates," Captain Stinky Beard said when we raced into his quarters.

"Ahoy, right back," I said.

He took one look at our excited faces and asked what was going on. But we were all too out of breath to tell him. So Inna grabbed his hand and pulled him over to the window instead.

"Sink me!" Captain Stinky Beard said. Then he smiled real wide. "It's me old muck mate Captain Dagger Dan's ship," he said.

"Aye," Vicky said.

"Aye, and our old muck parents' ship, too!" Aaron said.

Captain Stinky Beard rushed out onto

the deck. "Man the sails and turn the ship about," Captain Stinky Beard ordered. The crew got to work, and soon we were heading right for the *Bone Rattler*.

Aaron and Vicky started dancing around even though dancing wasn't very piratey. But they couldn't help it. They were too excited to see their mom and dad.

"Arrr, I can't wait to show off all the stuff we've learned!" Aaron said.

"What do you mean by *wait*? You're always showing off!" Vicky reminded him.

Aaron crossed his arms. "Yeah, but this time I have new stuff to show off," he said. "Like my swashbuckling skills!" Then he started leaping around and swinging his arms everywhere. He was so busy goofing around that he didn't see Rotten Tooth coming up the galley stairs.

BANG!

Aaron buckled Rotten Tooth right in the gut!

"ARRR!" Rotten Tooth growled through his green teeth.

"Arrr, I was just p-practicing," Aaron stuttered.

"I thought I ordered ye mangy pollywogs to repair the deck," Rotten Tooth barked.

Before we could answer, Captain Stinky Beard approached. Lucky for us, the cap'n was the boss of Rotten Tooth. Plus, he thought we were shipshape pirate kids and he didn't like it when Rotten Tooth bullied us around.

"I ordered our little shipmates to take

11

the day off from lessons," Captain Stinky Beard explained.

"Aye?" Rotten Tooth asked.

"Aye!" the cap'n said. Then he pointed out to sea at the *Bone Rattler*. "Avast, we're getting visitors today."

Rotten Tooth took one glance and then . . . he smiled!

I couldn't believe my eyes!

Rotten Tooth never, ever smiled.

"Arrr, is he feeling icky sicky?" Gary asked.

"Aye, he must be!" I whispered.

"Hogwash!" Aaron said. "Rotten Head is probably just happy to see his old sea pal, Peg Leg Pedro. He's the first mate on the *Bone Rattler*."

I reached under my pirate hat and scratched my head. "Aye?" I asked. "I didn't know Rotten Tooth had friends."

"Aye, it's a true fact," Vicky said.

"Aye! Peg Leg's the one who warned us not to make Rotten Tooth angry," Aaron added.

"Humpf!" Inna snorted. "If he warned you about Rotten Guts, how come you're always getting us in trouble?"

"Because his brain is waterlogged, that's why!" Vicky said.

We all laughed at that. Aaron was too excited to argue.

Once both ships were sailing side by side, two pirates came aboard the *Sea Rat*. One of them had black hair and a long black beard. He even wore a black hat with a dagger on it.

"That's Captain Dagger Dan," Vicky whispered.

"Aye, and that's Peg Leg Pedro," Aaron said. He pointed to a shorter pirate with one wooden leg.

Two more pirates came onto our ship after them. Only these pirates didn't look like strangers. One looked like Aaron, and

13

the other looked like Vicky. They even wore the same red-and-white striped outfits. They looked exactly like my mates, only these pirates were grown up all the way.

"AVAST!" Vicky shouted. "It's Mom and Dad!"

Aaron and Vicky raced off. Their parents scooped them up into a giant hug. When they put them back on the deck, Vicky and Aaron couldn't stand still. They ran around in circles, jumped up and down, and climbed on their parents like a pair of crazy monkeys!

"Arrr! Looks like Pirate School has tamed these two rascals," Captain Dagger Dan said when he saw Aaron and Vicky.

My eyes went all big, and my mouth fell open.

I looked at Gary and Inna. Their eyes were open real big, too!

"Blimey!" Inna said. "I wonder what they were like before."

"AYE!" Peg Leg Pedro said. Then he patted Aaron and Vicky on the head.

"These runts were as wild as a storm!"

"Well, we be awfully glad ye sent them here," Captain Stinky Beard said. "These shipmates have saved our tails more than once."

Rotten Tooth grumbled, but he couldn't say anything because it was the truth. We'd saved the ship a bunch of times.

"Arrr, I'm glad I came up with the idea to send them here," Aaron and Vicky's dad said.

"Arrr! It was *my* idea," their mom said.

"Was not."

"Was too!"

"Arrr, not only do they look like Aaron and Vicky," I whispered to Gary, "they also act like them."

"Aye!" Gary agreed.

As the ships sailed on, Aaron and Vicky took turns swapping tales with their parents. I listened as they told them all about our adventures at Pirate School. I liked those stories the best because I was always in them!

Chapter 3
Ship Leave

"ARRR! That be one whale of a tale," Captain Dagger Dan growled. He'd been listening to Vicky tell her parents about the time we saved the *Sea Rat* from a cursed treasure. "Ye wouldn't be yanking yer old captain's timbers, would ye?"

Vicky shook her head. "No, sir! It's a true whale tale!"

Dagger Dan didn't look so sure. He made his eyes go real small, and his mouth curled into a frown. Then he pointed at Aaron and Vicky. "Arrr, it wouldn't be the first time ye two muck mates told a fib," he said.

Inna marched over to him and crossed her arms. "Arrr! It's the whole truth," she huffed. "And I NEVER fib, so there!"

I shook my head. The tiniest bit of slime made Inna scream. But she wasn't afraid of big pirates!

Captain Dagger Dan tugged on his black beard and stared at Inna with angry eyes. I thought for sure he was going to make shark bait out of her! But before he could say anything, Peg Leg Pedro started laughing.

"Arrr! That's one tough little pup," Peg Leg said.

"Aye," Inna said with a big smile. "Tough and pretty!"

"Aye, but mostly tough," Gary said. "She bops me on the head at least once a day!"

Inna made a frowny face. "I wouldn't have to bop you at all if you weren't such a blunder head."

All of a sudden,

Captain Dagger Dan roared with laughter. "Okay, I believe you," he said. "I wouldn't want to get bopped on the head." Then he turned to Captain Stinky Beard and got all whispery. Captain Stinky Beard got all whispery right back.

I tried to hear what they were saying. It was no use.

As soon as they were done whispering, both captains turned back to us.

"Attention!" Captain Stinky Beard ordered.

Me and my mates lined up.

"Arrr, how would ye mates like to go on an away mission?" Captain Stinky Beard asked us.

"Blimey!" I shouted. "Only real brave pirates get to go on away missions!"

"Aye," Dagger Dan agreed. "And I would like ye brave pirates to spend one week on the *Bone Rattler* and prove yer guff."

"Aye? You mean like a test?" Gary asked.

"Aye!" Captain Stinky Beard said. "Do ye think yer ready?"

"Aye, aye!" we all shouted. Then we gave both of them a salute.

"Then it's all set," Captain Stinky Beard said. "Ye lot will join the crew of the *Bone Rattler*. In one week, both ships will dock at port and we'll take ye back aboard to see how ye faired."

"Yippee!" we cheered. We couldn't wait to prove what great pirates we were.

"Arrr, now go grab yer packs and be ready to board as soon as we raise anchor!" Captain Dagger Dan ordered.

"Double aye, aye!" we said.

Then we gave our pirate cheer.

"SWASHBUCKLING, SAILING, FINDING TREASURE, TOO! BECOMING PIRATES IS WHAT WE WANT TO DO!"

"That's the spirit, mateys!" Peg Leg Pedro bellowed.

"Aye," Rotten Tooth grumbled. "Just be sure not to let me down," he warned.

It sure was going to be nice not having him as our teacher for a week!

Chapter 4
Setting Sail!

"Arrr, I think we made a wrong turn," Gary said once we reached our guest quarters on the *Bone Rattler*.

"Aye! No pirate said anything about having to sleep in this dingy place," Inna said.

I took a look around.

The room had no portholes, and the bunks were covered with slimy gunk. I even had to pinch my nose because it smelled the teeniest bit like fish guts. "Aye," I said. "I think this might be a bathroom."

Just then, Aaron and Vicky came running into the quarters. They tossed their pillows onto the grimy bunks. Then they looked around and gave us a big smile.

"Arrr! Can you believe we get to spend a whole week on the *Bone Rattler*?" Aaron asked us.

"Aye!" Vicky said. "Plus, the cap'n gave us the best room on the ship!"

"Blimey! This is the best room on the ship?" Inna asked.

"Aye," Aaron said. "Pretty shipshape, huh?"

Gary took off his glasses and wiped them. After he put them back on, he took another peek around. "Arrr, I'm not sure Aaron knows what 'shipshape' means," he said to me.

"Aye," I said. "I'm not sure any pirate aboard does! The whole ship is rickety and rackety."

"Aye!" Inna said. "It's a miracle this pile of bones can even float!"

"It's a true fact," I said. "There are loose boards on every deck, and the galley stairs are even missing steps. Gary tripped and tumbled three times on the way down! Plus, the entire ship is even dirtier than a pile of dishes after a feast of seaweed slop!"

"Hogwash!" Aaron said, and waved his hand in the air. "Besides, none of that matters! This hunk of junk is the fastest ship on the seas."

"Aye," Vicky agreed. "Captain Dagger Dan might not run a tight ship, but it still sails, and that's all that counts."

I scratched my head and wrinkled my nose. "Mayhap," I said. "But I'm just not so sure it's a safe ship."

"Don't be such a worry whale," Aaron said.

"Aye, this week's going to be smooth sailing!" Vicky said.

"More like *filthy* sailing," Inna grumbled.

Just then, we heard Captain Dagger Dan order all hands on deck.

We hurried onto the main deck. The whole crew was there. There were tall pirates and short pirates and ugly pirates and really ugly pirates. Each one of them was dirtier than the next. Plus, they all smelled a little stinky. But that wasn't the

strange part. The strange thing was that
NONE of them were doing any chores!

"Arrr, this sure is one funny ship," I whispered to Gary.

"Aye," Gary whispered back.

Then Captain Dagger Dan ordered the crew to raise the sails. "We be setting a new course," he said.

"Arrr! Where're we headed, Cap'n?" Peg Leg Pedro asked.

Captain Dagger Dan closed one eye and tugged on his black beard. "ARRR! We be heading for treasure," he said. The crew cheered.

I let out a loud cheer, too. That's because hunting for treasure was my favorite pirate thing to do.

"There be a treasure not too far from here," Captain Dagger Dan told us. "No ship has ever dared to claim it because it be lost in the depths of Shipwreck Pass. But that won't stop us, will it, mates?"

The crew of the *Bone Rattler* cheered even louder than before. But I didn't cheer at all this time.

"Great sails," I said to my mates. "I don't

like the sound of that place."

"Aye!" Gary said. "I read all about Shipwreck Pass in my book of pirate tales. It said no ship has ever made it back from there in one piece."

Inna flashed Gary a mean look. Then she pulled his hat down over his ears and bopped him on the head. "What did I tell you about bringing up those scary stories?" she growled.

Gary fixed his glasses and rubbed the ouch off his head. "Arrr, you told me not to," he said.

"That's right! So take it back!" Inna shouted.

"Arrr! Don't get your sails in a bunch," Vicky said. "We'll be safe as seashells! The cap'n knows what he's doing."

"Aye," Aaron agreed. "This is going to be easy breezy!"

Sometimes Aaron could be a real know-it-all. This time, I hoped he really did know what he was talking about.

Chapter 5
Vacation at Sea

"Shiver me timbers," I said. That's because my timbers were shaking all over the place. The *Bone Rattler* was getting tossed around by even the smallest waves. It was like sailing through a storm even though the sea was calm.

"Arrr, we might sink before we even get to Shipwreck Pass!" Gary said. Inna crossed her arms and growled at him. Gary covered his head real quick before Inna had the chance to bop him again.

"Aye," I said. "Gary's right. This ship is in bad shape. We better start making repairs or we'll never stay afloat."

"Aye, aye!" Inna and Gary said.

"First, we should try to get some other

pirates to help us," I said.

"Aye," Gary said. "How about Aaron and Vicky?"

"Arrr," Inna growled. "Those two won't be any help. They're too busy running wild!"

I took a peek around the deck. I spied Aaron and Vicky. They were leaping over barrels and racing around the masts with Peg Leg Pedro and their parents.

"Aye, Inna's right," I said. Then I pointed to a group of pirates lazing around by the railing. They looked as strong as rocks, and each of them had their bandanas over their eyes for a nap. "Let's ask them," I said.

We got up next to them and had to cover our ears. They were snoring so loud, it sounded like thunder.

"Maybe we shouldn't wake them up," Gary said. "They don't look very nice. They might toss us overboard if we ruin their nap."

"Flaming fish guts!" Inna said. "They don't look so scary. Besides, it's their duty to get this ship in shape."

"Aye," I said. Then I tapped the biggest pirate on the shoulder. He moaned and groaned and opened one eye. Then I gulped because I saw he only had one eye! The other eye was made of black glass.

"Arrr?" he growled.

"He doesn't look so jolly," I whispered.

"I told you we should've let him get some shut-eye," Gary whispered back.

"Arrr, but we need their help," I said.

"Help with what?" the snoozy pirate roared.

We GULPED!

"Help—help fixing the ship," Inna stuttered.

"Hogwash! This ship's fine," the pirate mumbled. Then he closed his eye again. We asked each of the other pirates to help, but they all said the same thing.

"I guess we'll have to do it by ourselves," I said.

"Aye," Inna said. "I'll stitch up all the tiny rips in the sail."

"Good thinking," I said. "And me and Gary will hammer all these boards until they're solid."

Inna started stitching, and I started hammering. Gary started hammering, too, only he had to stop right away. That's because he hammered his pants to the deck by mistake and got stuck.

Aaron raced by and spied Gary trying to get loose. He held his belly and started

laughing. "Yo-ho-ho!" he bellowed. "Gary blundered himself to the deck."

"Aye?" Vicky shouted. She stopped playing, too, and took a peek at Gary. Then she put her hands over her mouth to cover a giggle.

"Arrr! Maybe if you two helped, Gary wouldn't be blundering all over the place!" Inna shouted.

Vicky put her hands on her hips and huffed. "Why are you doing chores, anyway?" she asked. "No other pirate is!"

"Aye!" Aaron said. "And Rotten Tooth isn't around to give us orders. You should play tag with us. Peg Leg is so slow, he'll never catch us!"

"Or get some shut-eye like the rest of the crew," Vicky added.

"Arrr! But it's our duty to take care of the ship," I said.

"Aye! Pete's right!" Inna said. "This ship's sure to end up at the bottom of sea if we don't do something!"

"Stow yer worries!" Vicky said. "This bucket of bolts is fine."

"AYE! MORE THAN FINE! IT'S THE BEST SHIP ON THE SEA!" a voice boomed behind me. I spun around real fast and saw Captain Dagger Dan standing there.

"Ahoy, Cap'n," I said.

"Ahoy to you," he said. "Ye mind telling me why yer mucking about with those hammers?"

"Just doing some fixing, Cap'n," I said. I couldn't tell him that we thought his ship was in sink shape. Captains didn't like it when pirate kids told them how to run their ship.

Dagger Dan bent down to look at me eye to eye.

I GULPED again!

He sure was a scary-looking pirate. Even in the daytime, his eyes were as black as the depths of the deepest sea! But then I had to rub my own eyes because I didn't believe what they were showing me. That scary pirate Captain Dagger Dan was smiling and patting me on the head!

"I didn't invite ye aboard to be deckhands," he said. "You lil' scoundrels are here to run amuck and have some fun!"

"HIP HIP HOORAY!" Aaron and Vicky shouted.

I wasn't so shouty, though. The ship was still in danger.

"But Cap'n," I said. "The pirate code says—"

"Fish feathers!" Captain Dagger Dan said before I could finish. "Now put those tools away and run wild! That be an order!"

"Aye, aye," I mumbled.

"See, I told you!" Aaron said once the captain left. "We don't have to do any of that stinky school stuff on this ship."

"I guess you're right," I said with a shrug.

"I'm always right!" Aaron said. And for once, he really was right.

"What are we going to do now, Pete?" Gary asked me.

"Sink me," I said. "I guess we should play. After all, orders be orders."

"Aye, that's the spirit!" Vicky said.

"Aye, let's play swashbuckling!" Aaron shouted. Then he picked up a mop and started swinging it around. If we were still on the *Sea Rat*, he would've been in big trouble. But here, we were allowed to buckle all we wanted.

And even though I was worried about the ship, I had to admit playing was a lot more fun than making repairs!

Chapter 6
Danger, Dead Ahead!

"Arrr! Don't look now, but Shipwreck Pass is dead ahead!" I shouted.

The ship was sailing toward a large island. There was a narrow passage that went right through the middle, and jagged rocks stuck out in every direction.

"Good eye, matey!" Peg Leg Pedro said with a big smile.

Inna covered her eyes. Then she spread her fingers apart to take a peek. "It looks spooky," she whispered.

"Aye," Gary agreed.

"There's nothing to be spooked about," Peg Leg told us. "This here's the finest crew and cap'n on the seas. We'll get in there and get out with the treasure."

"AYE!" Aaron and Vicky agreed.

I wasn't so sure.

I wrinkled my nose and looked around. I saw one group of pirates playing cards and another group taking turns spitting over the railing. I even saw two pirates having a food fight and slinging slop about. But I didn't see a single pirate working.

"I'll go tell the cap'n we've made it," Peg Leg said.

"Blimey! It looks like a ship graveyard!" Gary said once we were near enough to see the wrecks of a whole bunch of ships floating on the waves.

Inna reached over and yanked his hat over his ears. Then she gave him an extra-big bop on the head! "STOP SAYING SPOOKY STUFF!" she hollered.

"Arrr! But it's the truth," I said. "There must be one thousand hundred ships!" I wasn't sure exactly how many sunken ships were there because pirates aren't very good at counting. But I was sure one thousand hundred was a pretty good guess.

I kept glancing over my shoulder to see if the crew was paying attention. But they were all still mucking around.

"Arrr, those rocks are getting really close!" Gary said as the ship entered the pass. The jagged rocks were sticking out like sharp swords.

"Aye," Vicky said. "This doesn't look like such a good idea."

"Sink me! You're turning into a scallywag, too?" Aaron said.

"I'm no scallywag!" Vicky yelled. "But I don't want to turn into shark bait, either."

"Great sails!" Aaron said. "The cap'n knows what he's doing. You'll see!"

But the only thing I saw was a lot of sharp rocks getting closer and closer.

SMASH!

Then . . . CRASH!

The ship slammed right into one of the big rocks!

The whole entire ship wibbled and wobbled! It felt like the ship was going under.

"Let's go, mateys!" I said. "We'd better see if the crew needs our help!"

I thought the whole crew would be rushing about trying to keep us afloat. But when I turned around, they were all still too busy goofing off.

We hurried to find Aaron and Vicky's parents. We were sure they'd listen to us.

"Arrr! There you are!" Aaron and Vicky's mom said once she saw us. "We were just coming to fetch ye runts!"

"Aye?" Vicky asked. "So you are worried?"

"Aye! Worried as whales!" their dad said.

I wiped my forehead. "At least some pirates have come to their senses," I said.

"Aye!" their mom said. "The whole crew is getting set to sing a sea shanty without any pirates singing the chorus! That's where we need ye lot to lend yer pipes!"

I looked at my mates and made a funny face. They all made funny faces back at me. Those funny faces meant we were confused.

"Aye? The *whole* crew is going to sing?" Vicky asked.

"Aye! They're ready to burst," her dad said.

"Isn't any pirate checking the ship for damage?" I asked.

"Aye," Inna said. "We hit that rock pretty hard!"

"Gullyfluff!" their dad said. Then he crossed his arms and lifted his head high in the air. It was the same thing Aaron did whenever he thought someone was being silly.

"Aye!" their mom said. "First we sing, then we work."

"Arrr, this whole ship is crazy. We should check, anyway," I whispered to Vicky.

"Aye," Vicky whispered back. Then she told her parents we were going belowdecks. "We want to get some snacks before we sing," she said. She knew if she'd told them the truth, they'd order us to have fun instead.

"Aye, good thinking," I said once we were alone.

"Aye!" Aaron said. "I'm starving!"

"We're not really getting snacks, dodo brain!" Vicky said. "We're going to check on the ship."

"Arrr!" Aaron said.

Then we raced down the galley steps. Soon we were on the lowest deck of the ship. Only it wasn't really a deck anymore. It was more like a swimming pool!

"Sink me!" I shouted. "The ship has sprung a leak!"

Chapter 7
In a Fix

"Arrr! I'm not sure this is working," Gary said. He had his finger plugged in a hole, but water was still seeping into the ship.

"Aye!" I said. I was covering the one big hole with both hands and water was still spraying me in the face!

"Hold yer sea horses!" Aaron told us. "I'll have this water out in two shakes of a shark's tail!" He grabbed a bucket and started scooping the water up. Then he poured the water into a sink.

"ARRR! That's not going to do anything!" Vicky hollered.

"Will too!" Aaron said. "All the water will go down the drain, then this deck will be dry as a desert."

"Aye, but more water keeps spilling in!"
Gary said. By now, he was plugging one
hole with each hand and one with his foot.
He tried to plug another one with his nose,
but it only made him sneeze.

"Avast!" Inna shouted. "I fixed one of
them!" She was able to plug one little hole
with her hair ribbon.

"Aye, good work!" I said. "We can use our socks to plug up the tiny leaks."

"Aye, aye!" my mates shouted.

We took off our boots and shoved our socks into the tiny leaks. Then there was only the big hole left. But none of our socks were that big. Not even Rotten Tooth's socks would've been big enough to plug that hole!

"Soggy sails!" Vicky said. "Now what?"

"I know!" Aaron said. "We'll make another really big hole in the floor, then all the water will drain out!"

"You blunder head! That won't fix anything!" Vicky argued. "The water will keep raining in from the other hole!"

Aaron scratched his head. "Aye? I guess you're right," he admitted.

"I know! If it's raining, why don't we use an umbrella?" Gary said.

"Arrr, that's even dafter than Aaron's plan!" Vicky said.

I wiped the water off my forehead and thought about Gary's plan. "Arrr, maybe it's not so daft," I said.

"Aye?" Gary asked.

"Aye," I said.

"Pete, I think maybe you've gone a little daft," Aaron said.

"Not a chance," I said. "We can make a funny kind of umbrella and put it over the outside of that big hole. The water trying to get in will pull it tight to the ship and seal the leak. Then the ship will stay afloat."

"Aye! Just like when I have to patch up my pants whenever I tear them!" Gary said, and I nodded.

"Aye! It's an emergency trick that I learned about on my old ship," I said.

"That's good thinking, Pete!" Vicky said.

"Aye," Inna said. "But where are we going to find anything like that?"

"Aye, and how are we going to get to the outside of the ship?" Gary asked.

"Arrr, I haven't figured that part out," I said.

"I bet the cap'n can help," Vicky said.

"Aye," I said.

Even if Captain Dagger Dan didn't run a tight ship, he was still a real live pirate captain. And if there was one thing a pirate captain knew, it was how to save his ship! So we hurried back to the main deck as quickly as a flock of electric eels!

The deck was crowded with singing pirates. It was hard work pushing and shoving our way over to the ship's wheel, where the cap'n was.

"Captain, we have something very important to report," I said, but he didn't hear me. He was singing and shouting too loud.

"CAPTAIN!" Vicky yelled at the top of her lungs. She shouted so loud, I had to cover my ears, but the captain still didn't notice.

That's when Inna went up to him and tugged on his coat. Then she gave him a nudge. And when that didn't work, she gave him a swift poke in his belly!

"QUIET!" the captain roared, and the

whole crew hushed. "NOBODY POKES THE CAP'N!"

All eyes turned to us! Finally we had the crew's attention!

"But Cap'n . . . we have to tell you something," I said.

He looked us up and down.

"Blimey! Where have ye soggy sea pups been?" the cap'n asked. "You're dripping from head to tail!"

"Arrr! 'Tis not safe to swim without letting the cap'n know," Peg Leg Pedro scolded us. "I thought they would've taught ye that at Pirate School!"

Vicky put her hands on her hips and made a huff. "ARRR! We didn't go swimming! We went belowdecks!"

"Belowdecks!" Captain Dan shouted. "But that would mean we sprung a leak!"

"That's what we've been trying to tell you," I explained.

Before I could say anything else . . . WHAM!

The *Bone Rattler* was struck on both sides! It got stuck between two huge rocks and stopped sailing!

Suddenly every pirate's timbers started shaking and shivering. It was clear that the ship was sinking!

"Great stormy seas!" Captain Dagger Dan roared. "ALL HANDS ABANDON SHIP!"

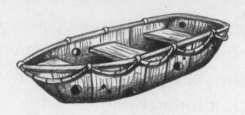

Chapter 8
Stuck in a Rut

The pirates on the ship raced in every direction. Some pirates even started climbing up the rigging like a bunch of monkeys. But not a single pirate went overboard.

"Arrr! Why aren't ye abandoning the ship like I ordered?" Captain Dagger Dan roared.

"Captain, we lowered the lifeboats, but they were so full of holes that they sank!" Peg Leg Pedro told him.

"Slimy slugs!" Cap'n Dan yelled in surprise. "It looks like our ship is really sunk this time!"

"But Cap'n, we can still save the ship," Vicky pleaded.

"Aye!" I said. "We have a plan, but we need your help."

Captain Dagger Dan wasn't really listening. He just kept pacing back and forth and rubbing his beard. "Sorry, matey! This be no time for wee pirate games," he said, and hurried away with Peg Leg.

"Arrr, it's no use," I told my mates. "We have to figure it out all by ourselves!"

"Aye!" my friends yelled.

Then we put our hands in a circle and said our pirate cheer.

"SWASHBUCKLING, SAILING, FINDING TREASURE, TOO! SAVING THE SHIP IS WHAT WE WANT TO DO!"

There was no time to waste, so we went right to work.

"First, we need something waterproof," I said.

We all looked around, but there was nothing waterproof anywhere on deck.

Suddenly, I had an idea!

"Inna? Did you bring a lot of clothes like you always do?" I asked.

"Aye," Inna said. "I brought all my prettiest outfits."

"Is one of them a raincoat?" I asked.

Inna tapped her chin and thought. Then her eyes got real big. "AYE! It's my pink one with purple polka dots. It's my favorite! Oh, and it's waterproof!" she said. "I'll go get it!"

"Arrr, now we need a rope ladder, four pegs, and a hammer," I said.

"Aye!" Vicky said. "I know where the hammers are."

"I know where to get a rope ladder!" Aaron said.

"And I know where we can get pegs," Gary said. "I tripped over them on the way over here."

Soon, everyone was back with the supplies we needed.

"Arrr! Now what?" Aaron asked.

"Now we toss a rope ladder over the railing," I explained. "I'll climb down and patch up the hole with Inna's coat. Then I'll nail it into place."

"Arrr, no one said anything about pounding nails in my coat!" Inna growled.

"Would you rather sink?" Vicky asked.

Inna made a frown. "Fine!" she huffed. "But someone is getting me a new coat if we make it out of this mess!"

I raced over to the railing and started to climb down. Aaron and Vicky held the ladder steady. Gary had his head poked over the side to guide me. Inna was supposed to help him, but she was too scared to look.

I took a peek below me. The waves were splishing and splashing all over the place and all over me. I had to wipe the water away so I could see. Then I saw the hole just under the water's surface!

I climbed down a few more steps and got into place.

"That's it, Pete! You can do it!" Gary shouted.

"Aye! I better do it fast!" I shouted back. I slipped Inna's raincoat out from under my arm. I tried sliding it over the hole, but the water was rushing so fast, it almost took the coat with it.

"Hammer the top corners first," Gary shouted.

"Good thinking," I yelled. Gary might be clumsy, but he sure was a smart pirate.

I hammered the top two corners in place. Then I pulled the bottom two over the hole.

Then . . . GLUG!

The water stopped rushing in. The sea was pushing the coat so hard that it held tight to the ship. I hurried up and hammered the last two corners before it could slip out of place!

I glanced above me and gave Gary the thumbs-up.

"It worked! It worked!" Gary shouted as I climbed back onto the deck.

I wiped my forehead. "That was a close one!"

"Aye," Vicky said. "The closest one ever."

"Arrr, I wasn't worried," Aaron said. "I knew the plan would work all along!"

We were all too tired to argue with him. We just rolled our eyes and shook our heads.

"Arrr! I guess we should go find our parents and let them know we're still sailing," Vicky told her brother.

"Arrr, and we should let the cap'n know the ship isn't sinking anymore," Inna told me and Gary.

"Aye," I agreed. Then I made a grumpy face. "But I'm going to miss watching all the grown-ups run around like a bunch of monkeys!"

Chapter 9
SOS

"Three cheers for our lil' shipmates!" the crew hollered once we told them that the ship wasn't sinking.

"Shipshape work, mateys!" Captain Dagger Dan told us. "I never would've thought of using a raincoat to patch up a ship."

We smiled really proud. Saving the ship was the best thing a pirate could do, besides finding treasure of course.

"There's still one problem," I said.

"Aye?" Vicky asked.

"Aye!" I said. "The ship is still STUCK!"

The whole crew made *oohs* and *aahs*. They were so happy we hadn't sunk that they forgot all about being stuck.

The crew all looked toward Captain

Dagger Dan. He rubbed his chin and looked out to sea.

Then the cap'n shook his head. "The only way out of this rut is if another ship gives us a tug from behind. And no other pirate cap'n be brave enough to try their luck on Shipwreck Pass," he said.

"Brave?" Inna whispered in my ear. "Arrr, I think he meant to say 'crazy' instead."

The crew moaned and groaned. It looked like there was no way out of this.

"This stinks!" I said. "We'll never get to be real pirates if we're stuck in this floating graveyard forever."

"Aye," Aaron said. "I say this stinks worse than sinking."

"Aye, me too," Gary said. "It stinks worse than rotting sea slugs!"

"Me three," Vicky said. "It stinks worse than Rotten Tooth's breath!"

"We can't give up yet," I said. "If we give up, we'll never see the *Sea Rat* again. I don't care what the cap'n says—we should start a signal fire. There's still a chance a ship will be close enough to see it!"

"ARRR!" a voice roared behind me. I spun around and saw the cap'n staring down at me. "ARE YE QUESTIONING ME ORDERS?" he growled. Captains didn't like it when pirate kids questioned their orders. If I hadn't just helped to save the ship, he might have made me walk the plank.

"Aye," I whispered.

Dagger Dan squinted at me and leaned so close to me that I stumbled backward. When I caught my balance, he didn't look so mad anymore.

"Do ye know how to make a signal fire?" he asked, and I nodded. "Then by all means, get to work, sailor! I ignored ye runts once—I won't be doing it again!"

"Aye, Cap'n!" I said. Then I gave him a big salute.

We perked right up and started gathering planks for the fire. Then the cap'n ordered every pirate to help us. Soon, the whole ship was hard at work for the first time since we set sail.

"If we make it out of this, I'm giving ye a rich reward!" Captain Dagger Dan whispered to me.

I smiled really, really, really wide! Then I crossed my fingers and double-hoped that a ship would sail our way. First, I wanted to be saved. And second, I really wanted that reward!

Chapter 10
Safe at Last

I kept watch all afternoon, but I didn't see any ships.

"Rotten fish guts," Vicky said. "We're never getting saved!"

I looked around the deck. Even the bravest pirates on board were moping! "We need some good news to raise our spirits," I whispered to my mates.

"Aye," Gary agreed.

I went back to watching the sea. It wasn't long before something caught my eye way out on the waves. I took out my spyglass and spied through it.

"Blow me down!" I shouted. "A ship! And it's heading this way!"

"Let me see!" Aaron shouted. He took the spyglass and peeked through it. "Pete's right! There's a ship!"

Vicky took the spyglass from him so she could see for herself. "Great sails!" she shouted. "It's the *Sea Rat*!"

"They must have seen the signal fire," Gary said.

"Yippy skippy! We're rescued!" Inna shouted.

She was right, too!

The *Sea Rat* steered into Shipwreck Pass. Soon, it was right on our tail. I saw Captain Stinky Beard on deck and waved. "Ahoy, Cap'n!" I shouted.

"Ahoy!" he shouted back. "Looks to me like ye need a tow."

"Aye!" I said.

Then I reported to Captain Dagger Dan, and he ordered the crew to toss the ropes over to the *Sea Rat*. Soon, both ships were latched together.

Then Rotten Tooth and Captain Stinky Beard came aboard.

"Thanks for saving our tails," I told Captain Stinky Beard.

"Arrr! It be Rotten Tooth ye should thank," Captain Stinky Beard told him. "He kept us on a close course. He heard rumor of a treasure buried at the bottom of Shipwreck Pass and figured Dagger Dan would try to find it."

"Aye?" Inna asked. "Does that mean you were worried about us?"

Rotten Tooth turned a little red. "I was worried about my mate Peg Leg, not ye barnacles," he mumbled, but we could tell he was fibbing. He didn't like to admit it, but we knew that deep down, he sort of liked us a teeny-tiny bit.

"Arrr," Captain Dagger Dan said. "Ye were right not to worry about this lot. These pollywogs saved our ship! If it weren't for them, we'd be at the bottom of the sea!"

"Aye," Peg Leg agreed. "These runts will

make shipshape captains one day."

"Aye!" Captain Stinky Beard agreed.

Me and my mates smiled and clapped our hands. Hand clapping wasn't very piratey, but we were too happy to care.

"I only wish we'd found that treasure," Captain Dagger Dan said. "Then we could pay them back. If ye like, yer welcome to stay on until we find another treasure," he told us.

"Aye, ye still have a few days of vacation," Rotten Tooth said.

We all shook our heads back and forth really fast.

"Thanks, but no thanks," I said.

"Aye," Inna said. "I think we need a vacation from our vacation!"

Both captains roared with laughter.

We gathered our things as quick as we could and hurried back on deck. Vicky and Aaron said good-bye to their parents. That took a long time because they all started arguing about who was going to miss who the most.

Then Captain Stinky Beard and Dagger Dan ordered both crews to reverse the sails.

The *Bone Rattler* creaked and squeaked.

Then . . . WHOOSH!

It was sailing once again!

As soon as we pulled away from the rocks, I noticed something shiny in the water. I raced over to the railing and peered at the bottom of the sea.

"AVAST!" I shouted. "THE TREASURE!"

The entire crew ran over and looked into the clear water. There was treasure littered all over the place!

"Looks like we found the treasure after all," Vicky said.

"Aye! I told you we would," Aaron said.

The best swimmers on both ships dove in to gather it.

Once all the treasure was safely on deck, Captain Dagger Dan took his share. Then he handed it over to me and my mates!

"I'll be giving my share to these runts," he said.

We couldn't believe our eyes!

A whole captain-sized treasure just for us!

"Blimey! We must be the richest pirate kids on the sea," Gary said.

"Aye!" I agreed. I'd never had so much treasure in my whole entire life. But that wasn't even the happiest part of the day. The happiest part was when we set sail again on the *Sea Rat* and waved good-bye to our new friends!

"Arrr, it's nice to be rich, but it's even nicer to be home," I told my mates.

"Aye!" Gary said.

"Double aye!" Inna said. "Getting bossed around by Rotten Tooth beats sailing in a rickety ship like the *Bone Rattler*!"

Even Vicky and Aaron had to agree.

"I like the *Bone Rattler*," Vicky said, "but Rotten Tooth has a point about keeping up on repairs."

"Aye," Aaron said. "Keeping the ship in top-notch shape means the mess hall never floods!"

We all giggled. Then we rubbed our bellies—we were starving! We hadn't had a thing to eat on that ship! Our next Pirate School lesson could wait until we'd finished stuffing our faces. After all, we *were* on vacation!